Iris and Walter
Lost and Found

Iris and Walter
Lost and Found

WRITTEN BY

Elissa Haden Guest

ILLUSTRATED BY

Christine Davenier

Green Light Readers
Houghton Mifflin Harcourt
Boston   New York

For Louise, pal, painter, pilot extraordinaire—E.H.G.

For Henry Desmet, my favorite baby—C.D.

Text copyright © 2004 by Elissa Haden Guest
Illustrations copyright © 2004 by Christine Davenier

First Green Light Readers edition, 2014

The text of this book was set in Fairfield Medium.
The display type was set in Elroy.
The illustrations were created in pen-and-ink on keacolor paper.

The Library of Congress has cataloged the hardcover edition as follows:
Guest, Elissa Haden
Iris and Walter, lost and found/written by Elissa Haden Guest; illustrated by Christine Davenier
p. cm.
Summary: Iris's baby sister Rose breaks a necklace and is then discovered
playing with Walter's missing harmonica.
[1. Babies—Fiction. 2. Sisters—Fiction. 3. Lost and found possessions—Fiction.
4. Necklaces—Fiction. 5. Harmonica—Fiction.]
I. Title: Lost and found. II. Davenier, Christine, ill.
III. Title. PZ7.G9375Ism 2004
[E]—dc21 2002156518

ISBN: 978-0-15-216701-1 hardcover
ISBN: 978-544-22789-7 paperback

Manufactured in China
SCP 15 14 13 12 11

4500796236

Contents

1. Bad Rosie

Iris's little sister, Baby Rose, was a handful.

She crawled like the wind.

She climbed like a monkey.

She threw like a wild pitcher.

"You can't take your eyes off Baby Rose for a minute," said Iris's mother.
"She's one busy baby," said Iris's father.

One morning, Iris made a necklace
out of lovely old buttons.
"I'm going to bring this to school
for show-and-tell," said Iris.
"YA, YA!" said Baby Rose.

Baby Rose reached for Iris's necklace and grabbed it tight with her little fist.

"Let go, Rosie!" cried Iris.

But Baby Rose did not let go.

Baby Rose pulled and pulled.

Snap! Iris's necklace broke.

All the buttons scattered to the floor.

"Oh no!" cried Iris. "Bad Rosie!"

"She's just a baby," said Iris's father.

"She didn't mean to break it," said Iris's mother. "I'll help you fix it. It will be as good as new."

"No, it won't!" wailed Iris.

"Come along, my girl," said Grandpa. "You don't want to be late for school."

Iris stomped, stomped, stomped all the way to school. "Good morning, Iris," said Miss Cherry. But Iris did not think it was a good morning at all.

2. Show-and-Tell

"Hey, Iris, come sit with me!"
said Iris's best friend, Walter.
"I like your necklace," said Benny.
"Me, too," said Lulu.

"Today it is Iris's turn to begin
show-and-tell," said Miss Cherry.
Iris showed the class her button necklace.
"Now that's what I call a one-of-a-kind
necklace, Iris," said Miss Cherry.
Iris smiled.

Then it was Walter's turn.

"This was my grandma's harmonica,"
said Walter.

"My grandma taught my mother how to play
it, and now my mother is teaching me.
And tomorrow, my grandma is coming
to visit and *I'm* going to play it for her."

"Isn't that exciting," said Miss Cherry.

"Would you like to play a song
   for the class?" she asked.

"Okay," said Walter. He played
"Mary Had a Little Lamb."

"Wow, that was great," said Iris. "Can you teach me how to play the harmonica?"

"Sure!" said Walter.

After school, Iris and Walter climbed to their tree house for the harmonica lesson.

Iris *loved* playing the harmonica.

"This is so much fun," said Iris. "I might be a
musician when I grow up."

"We can both be musicians!" said Walter.

"Wait till I tell Grandma. Hey, do you want to
come over tomorrow and meet her?"
asked Walter.

"Sure!" said Iris.

When it was time to go home,

Iris asked, "Can I borrow your harmonica?"

"Well . . . ," said Walter.

"Please," said Iris. "I promise I'll bring it

back tomorrow.

"Okay, but just for tonight," said Walter.

"Thanks," said Iris.

Iris couldn't wait to play
the harmonica for her family.
"Well, listen to you!" said Iris's mother.
"It's 'Mary Had a Little Lamb'!"
said Iris's father.
"How terrific," said Grandpa.
Baby Rose thought it was terrific, too.

3. A Mystery

The next morning, after breakfast,

Iris packed her books and her lunch.

But when she went to pack

Walter's harmonica, it was gone.

"I can't find Walter's harmonica," said Iris.

"It has to be here," said Iris's mother.

"You were just playing it last night,"
  said Iris's father.

Iris and her father looked under the table

and behind the sofa

and inside the toy box. But they could not
find Walter's harmonica anywhere.

"What am I going to do?" cried Iris.

"I promised Walter I'd bring it *today!*"

"We'll find it, my Iris," said Iris's mother.

"It didn't run away by itself," said Iris's father.

"But where is it? Baby Rose, did you take
Walter's harmonica?" asked Iris.
Baby Rose said, "BLA, BLA."
"Give it back," said Iris.
"BLA, BLA, BLA!" shouted Baby Rose.

"Now, now, it's time for school, Iris,"
said Grandpa.

"I can't go to school!" said Iris. "I *have* to
find Walter's harmonica."

"Iris, my love, just tell Walter we are still
looking for it," said Iris's mother.

"I'm sure it will turn up," said Iris's father.

But what if it didn't turn up?

What if Walter's harmonica was lost forever?

4. Lost and Found

Iris walked slowly, slowly up the steps to school.

Walter was waiting for her.

"My grandma's going to pick us up from
school today," said Walter. "She can't wait to
meet you."

"Oh," said Iris. "Walter, I have something
terrible to tell you. I can't find your
harmonica."

"You can't?" Walter asked.

"No. But I *know* it's in my house somewhere."

"Did you look everywhere?" asked Walter.

"Everywhere," said Iris. "But I know it will
turn up."

"Today?" asked Walter.

"I hope so," said Iris.

It has to, she thought.

It was a very long day.

After school, Walter raced outside to meet
his grandma.
Iris walked slowly, slowly after him.

"Granny, this is Iris," said Walter.

"Iris, it's so good to meet you at last!"
said Walter's grandma.

Walter told his grandma about the lost
harmonica.

What if she gets mad? Iris held her breath.

"Iris, dear, would you like
us to help you look for it?"
asked Walter's grandma.

"Oh yes," said Iris.

"Thank you."

As they were walking up the path,
Iris heard a familiar sound.
She raced up the steps.

There was Baby Rose, sitting on the floor, blowing on the harmonica.

"You found it!" shouted Iris.

"It was in the laundry basket," said Iris's mother.

"And I think I know who put it there," said Iris's father.

"Hooray!" said Walter.

"Time for tea," said Grandpa.

"And a concert!" said Iris.

Everyone had a merry time

clapping and singing and dancing . . .

especially Baby Rose.